HECKEDY PEG

by Audrey Wood   Illustrated by Don Wood

Published by Child's Play (International) Ltd

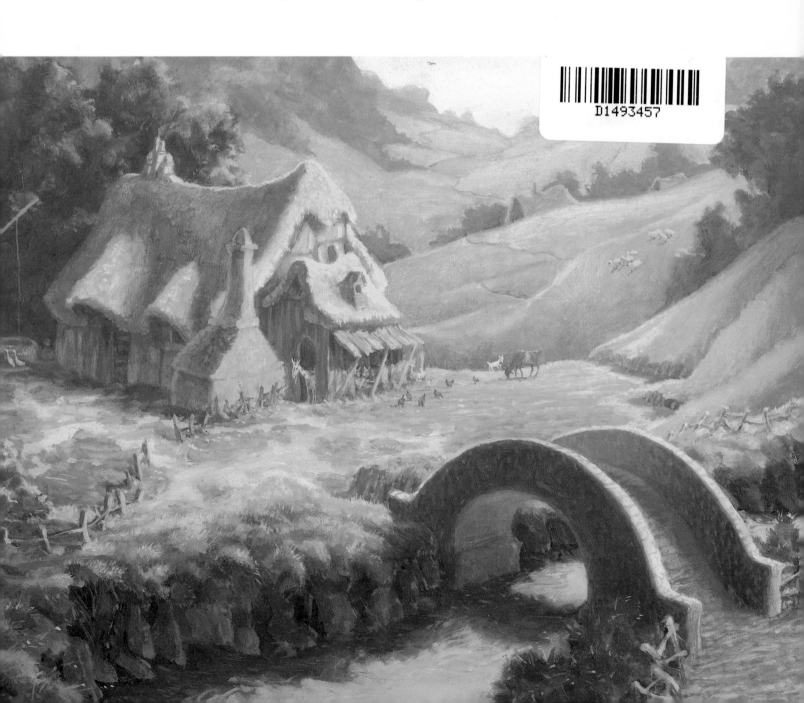

For Betty Smith Wood

Published by arrangement with Harcourt Brace Jovanovich, Inc.

Printed in Singapore

ISBN 0-85953-341-7

Down the dusty roads
and far away, a poor mother
once lived with her seven children
named Monday, Tuesday,
Wednesday, Thursday, Friday,
Saturday and Sunday.

Every day, before the mother
went to market, her children
helped with all the chores.

One morning, when they were
finished, the mother said,
"Because you are such good children,
you may ask for anything
you want and I will bring it home
from the market."

The children were overjoyed
and knew exactly what they wanted.

Monday asked for a tub of butter.

Thursday asked for a pot of honey.

Friday asked for a tin of salt.

Tuesday asked for a pocket knife.

Wednesday asked for a china jug.

Saturday asked for biscuits.

And Sunday asked for a bowl
of Yorkshire pudding.

The mother kissed her children
good-bye and said,
"Now be careful, and remember—
don't let a stranger in
and don't touch fire."
The children locked the door
behind her and began to play.

Before long, a witch hobbled up the road pulling a heavy cart.
She rapped at the window and called out:

"I'm Heckedy Peg.
I've lost my leg.
Let me in!"

"We can't," Monday, Tuesday, Wednesday, Thursday, Friday, Saturday
and Sunday called. "Mother told us not to let a stranger in."

Heckedy Peg took a pipe from her cape and stuck it in her mouth.

"Come now, sweet chickens," she called. "All I need is a light for my pipe.
Bring me a burning straw."

"We can't," Monday, Tuesday, Wednesday, Thursday, Friday, Saturday and Sunday called. "Mother told us not to touch fire."

Heckedy Peg reached in her cart and pulled out a sack.

"I'm sure your mother won't mind," she said. "Look! If you let me in and light my pipe, I'll give you this."

Leaning out of the window, the children looked into the sack. They couldn't believe their eyes.

"Gold!" they cried. "For a sack of gold we'll let you in and light your pipe."

The children unlocked the door and let the witch in.

They ran to the hearth and brought back burning sticks of straw to light her pipe.

But when it was lit,
Heckedy Peg threw the pipe
to the floor and shouted,
"Now I've got you!"

And with that the witch
turned the children into food.

Monday became bread.

Tuesday became pie.

Wednesday became milk.

Thursday became porridge.

Friday became fish.

Saturday became cheese.

And Sunday became
roast rib.

Heckedy Peg gathered up the food and loaded it in her cart.
Without looking back, she pulled the cart down the road,

over the bridge, through the town, across the field, and deep into the woods to her hut.

Soon the mother returned home carrying
a large basket. In it were all the things
her children wanted:
a tub of butter for Monday,
a pocket knife for Tuesday,
a china jug for Wednesday,
a pot of honey for Thursday,
a tin of salt for Friday,
biscuits for Saturday,
and a bowl of Yorkshire pudding
for Sunday.

"Monday, Tuesday, Wednesday,
Thursday, Friday, Saturday and Sunday!"
she called, but no one answered.

The mother found the witch's broken pipe
and burnt pieces of straw on the floor.
Tears flowed from her eyes.

"Who has taken my children?" she cried.

A blackbird who had seen everything
took pity on the mother and hopped down
to the windowsill.

"Follow me!" the bird chirped.
     "It's Heckedy Peg.
     She's lost her leg.
     They let her in."
Grabbing her basket, the mother followed
the blackbird down the road, over the bridge,
through the town, across the field, and deep
into the woods to the witch's hut.

Heckedy Peg had just sat down to supper and was about to

take her first bite when she heard a loud knock at the door.

"Let me in!" the mother called.
"I want my children back!"
    "You can't come in!"
said Heckedy Peg.
"Your shoes are dirty."
    "Then I'll take them off,"
the mother said, and so she did.
    "Let me in!" the mother called.
"I want my children back!"

    "You can't come in!"
said Heckedy Peg.
"Your socks are dirty."
    "Then I'll take them off,"
the mother said, and so she did.
    "Let me in!" the mother called.
"I want my children back!"
    "You still can't come in!"
said Heckedy Peg.
"Your feet are dirty."

"Then I'll cut them off," the mother said, and she went away
as if to do so. But instead, the mother hid her legs behind her
and crawled back to the witch's door.

"Let me in!" the mother called. "I want my children back!"

When Heckedy Peg looked down, she thought the mother had no feet,
so she let her in.

The witch pointed to the table.

"Here are your children," she said. "If you can't guess them right the first time, I'll eat them for my supper."

Keeping her feet tucked beneath her, the mother crawled to the table. How would she ever guess which food was which child?

In despair, the mother looked in her basket. *Here are the things my children wanted*, she thought, *and now they will never have them.*

"Hurry!" said the witch, "I'm hungry."

The mother looked at the food on the table.

"Speak up!" said the witch. "My supper grows cold."

Suddenly the mother knew what to do.
Taking the things from her basket, she said,
"I know my children by what they want."
   "Bread wants butter. That's Monday.
   "Pie wants knife. That's Tuesday.
   "Milk wants jug. That's Wednesday.
   "Porridge wants honey. That's Thursday.
   "Fish wants salt. That's Friday.
   "Cheese wants biscuits. That's Saturday.
   "And roast rib wants Yorkshire pudding.
That's Sunday."

Quick as a wink, the children turned back into themselves.

They hugged and kissed their mother, then hugged and kissed each other.

Jumping to her feet, the mother cried, "I've got my children back, Heckedy Peg. Now you'll be sorry you ever took them!"

She chased the witch around the hut, out of the woods,
across the field, through the town, and onto the bridge.

And Heckedy Peg jumped off the bridge and was never seen again.